DATE DUE

APR O~Y 199 N.M. 26			

Frozen Dinners

Strange Matter™
titles in Large-Print Editions:

Frozen Dinners

Johnny Ray Barnes, Jr.

Gareth Stevens Publishing
MILWAUKEE

For a free color catalog describing Gareth Stevens' list of high-quality books and
multimedia programs, call 1-800-542-2595 (USA) or 1-800-461-9120 (Canada).
Gareth Stevens Publishing's Fax: (414) 225-0377.
See our catalog, too, on the World Wide Web: http://gsinc.com

Library of Congress Cataloging-in-Publication Data

Barnes, Johnny Ray.
    Frozen dinners / by Johnny Ray Barnes, Jr.
      p. cm. -- (Strange matter)
    Summary: Left alone in the mountain home of their uncle during a blizzard,
  three children struggle against an attack by abominable snowmen who attempt
  to break into the house.
    ISBN 0-8368-1674-9 (lib. bdg.)
    [1. Ghosts--Fiction. 2. Yeti--Fiction. 3. Blizzards--Fiction. 4. Horror stories.]
  I. Title. II. Series.
PZ7.B26235Fr 1996
[Fic]--dc20   96-19609

This edition first published in 1996 by
Gareth Stevens Publishing
1555 North RiverCenter Drive, Suite 201
Milwaukee, Wisconsin 53212 USA

© 1995 by Front Line Art Publishing. Under license from Montage Publications,
a division of Front Line Art Publishing, San Diego, CA.

Printed in the United States of America

1 2 3 4 5 6 7 8 9 99 98 97 96

TO OUR FAMILIES
&
FRIENDS
(You know who you are)

"See anything out there, Max?" Uncle Shoe asked.

As I looked out the window at the forest surrounding my uncle's mountain home, I noticed it was the first morning since we'd arrived that everything wasn't covered in fog.

"It's so clear outside. I can see everything," I said, my breath clouding the window.

Uncle Shoe's big, two story home stood on one of the highest parts of the mountain, with no neighbors in sight. He lived by himself, but he always seemed very happy.

"You timed your vacation just right." Uncle Shoe stood up from his chair and lit his pipe. I heard him chuckle a little as he walked up behind me. "It's always this still before a little snow falls. You'll get in some sledding this week after all."

"Snow? Well, that blasts our hiking trip tomorrow," Mark, my older brother, whined. He sat on the floor, with Uncle Shoe's old radio torn into a thousand parts scattered across an old blanket. It had died just a couple of days before Mark, my sister Teresa, and I came up to stay. My brother's an electronics genius, so my uncle left the radio for him to fix.

The visit to Uncle Shoe's was my mother's idea. He's her older brother, and she's always worried about him getting lonely. She even nicknamed him 'Shoe' when they were younger, in hopes that it would take the place of his real name, Schubert, and make him more acceptable to people. But it didn't really work. Uncle Shoe simply liked his own company, and that was enough for him. Still, he always enjoyed seeing us, and seemed to really appreciate the visits.

Crier Mountain, where Uncle Shoe lives, is far enough away from Fairfield to make it seem like another world, but still close enough for Mom and Dad to send us there without worrying too much. Mom thought it would be nice if we spent a few days of our winter vacation in the mountains. Uncle Shoe doesn't get much company, but he's one of the nicest people I know, and he cares a lot for our whole family.

"The snow'll go soft in a day or so, Mark," said Uncle Shoe. "Plenty of time to walk this mountain. 'Til then you can hit the slopes with Max, or get that old transistor working."

"What about Teresa? Snowy weather could mess up that cell phone signal really nicely." Mark grinned, and pointed a screwdriver over in Teresa's direction.

Since we arrived at the cabin, she hadn't taken her ear away from Mom and Dad's cellular phone for more than an hour. Even now she sat crumpled on the couch with her feet in the air, gabbing like she got paid for it.

"Tyler Webb's cute, but he's too young for me. He's Max's age. A sixth grader. Nope, someone like Daniel Meeker is more my type. And by the way, Mark, if it snows, I can entertain myself very well, thank you."

I think she and Mark both have screws loose. Why else would they complain about snow? It never piles up as deep in Fairfield as it does in the mountains. We were in the perfect spot to enjoy it.

"Uncle Shoe, seriously, do you think it will snow tonight?" I felt myself shaking a little with excitement. Sure I liked hiking. Sure I liked getting to know nature. Sure I loved listening to Uncle Shoe's stories.

But above all else, I wanted a chance to go sledding.

Shooting down hills at top speed, right on the ragged edge of losing control. Isn't that what snow is for?

Uncle Shoe once told me that when he was a kid, they'd drive from Fairfield to Crier Mountain just to hit the wildest, roughest slopes around.

That was all I needed to hear.

I'd tamed my skateboard and mastered stump-jumping on my bike. But hard-core sledding was untouched territory for me. Mom always says I'm too much of a daredevil, but if things aren't a little scary, they're just no fun.

"Max," Uncle Shoe said, "I can say with a great amount of certainty that when you wake up tomorrow morning, you will see a little snow. I feel it in my bones. The question is, what are you going to use to tackle the hills?"

"I've got an inner tube in my suitcase. A big

4

yellow one."

Uncle Shoe's nose crinkled.

"You want to go sledding in a big yellow dough-nut? My boy, to go sledding, you need *a sled*."

Stepping over Mark's wiry mess on the floor, he made his way over to a corner closet. From the way the door popped when he opened it, you would have thought it'd been glued shut for years. After looking through the stuff inside for a few seconds, Uncle Shoe grabbed for some-thing deep inside.

He pulled out an old wooden sled.

"I call it Thunder Blades. It's yours to use if you can clean it up a bit."

"Sure thing! Thanks!" It looked like a molded piece of wood with two large butter knives attached on the bottom. And it had a lousy name. But I didn't want to hurt Uncle Shoe's feelings. Besides, I'd try anything once.

Then while I was looking it over, I found something.

Scarring the belly of the sled were long, deep cuts in the wood.

I couldn't be sure, but they looked like claw marks.

2

"Did a mountain lion come after you?" I asked.

Uncle Shoe looked as if he remembered something, but then scratched his head. "To tell you the truth, I'm not sure where those came from. There was a big storm here about fifty years ago and my friends and I hit the hills the day the snow let up. I took on a hill just around the way that we called 'The Cut.' You always wanted to make The Cut, which is off limits to you by the way. Anyway, on one of my runs, something hit the bottom of my sled. I crashed hard and Thunder Blades came out from under me. When I found her, she had those marks in her. Never did see the animal that made them, though. We found tracks of . . . something. After that, we never hit 'The Cut' again."

My eyes widened a bit.

"See, Max?" Teresa was actually talking to me instead of the phone. "If you go sledding, they'll get ya!"

"I hope that phone dies," I shot back. Teresa opened her mouth in horror, like I had just cursed her for life.

"Kids. Please. Now, do any of you want to go into town with me?" Uncle Shoe put his voice into a disciplinary tone as he searched for his coat and hat.

"What are you getting?" I asked.

"Just some groceries to fill the cupboards. If it snows more than a few inches, we won't be going into town for a couple of days. But hey, we'll make a party of it!"

"Then pick me up some crossword books please! I've finished all of mine," Teresa almost yelled. She usually solved all of her crosswords within the first two hours of any trip.

"No problem. Mark, any special requests?"

"Batteries. I need batteries for my alarm clock, Uncle Shoe. You don't have any here."

"Out again? Okay. More batteries. Max,

7

would you like to go?" he asked.

I looked down at the prehistoric sled in my hands.

"I think I'm going to start whipping Thunder Blades into shape. That way, I'll be ready to go first thing in the morning."

"So all of you kids are staying, eh? Well if you're all busy, that's fine. I'm only going to be in town for an hour or so anyway. Now, be sure and call your parents and let them know everything's okay. I'll be back shortly. And Max, get that sled into top shape because the snow's coming, I'm telling you."

I gave him a nod. Within a few moments, he had jumped into his truck and was driving slowly down the narrow mountain driveway.

Sitting down with the old sled and a couple of rags, I started cleaning, although I suspected all the cleaning in the world wouldn't help Thunder Blades. It took ten minutes of hard scrubbing to see underneath the layer of dirt covering the old wood.

Suddenly, a piercing whine came from the radio Mark had been slaving over. It quickly turned into a long electronic whistle.

"I did it! I did it! I've finally gotten this thing to make some noise," Mark yelled, turning the radio toward us.

Teresa clicked off the phone and laid it down. "Turn the dial. See if you can get a rock station on that thing!"

Mark searched with the dial until he found a spot free of static.

"AND THE CLOUDS ARE MOVING IN . . ."

"A lousy weather channel," Teresa said.

"Wait . . . " I wanted to hear about the snow.

"EVERYONE PREPARE TO SIT BACK AND WAIT THIS ONE OUT. NOT IN FIFTY YEARS HAVE WE SEEN A SNOW FRONT LIKE THIS ONE. IT'S A STORM THAT THIS WEATHER FORECASTER DOESN'T MIND CALLING A BLIZZARD. I CAN'T SAY EXACTLY WHICH PART OF THE COUNTY WILL BE HIT THE HARDEST, BUT I CAN SAY THAT IF YOU'RE IN THE MOUNTAIN AREA, YOU'RE GOING TO BE SNOWED IN . . ."

A blizzard.

Not a light snow like my uncle had thought, but a full fledged blizzard.

The biggest one in fifty years.

Teresa waited for us to confirm the weather on other radio stations before telling us about the phone.

She couldn't get it to work anymore.

Bad news. That was the only phone we had. Uncle Shoe didn't like the things at all. He always told us it would cost him too much to get phone lines run up the mountain, but I suspected that they just bothered him. He didn't like to have his peace interrupted by blaring rings.

"You've been talking on that thing ever since we got here," Mark scolded. "I knew that was coming. It's dead."

I remembered what I'd said to Teresa about the phone. A knot of guilt developed in the pit of my stomach.

"We can just recharge it," I said hopefully.

"We forgot to bring the AC adapter . . . ," Mark said.

"It runs on batteries," Teresa countered.

"And Uncle Shoe is out of batteries. I've already checked because I forgot to bring some myself. I knew this would happen, Teresa. You're a talking head."

"Hey, just because I have friends and you don't . . ."

I'd heard all of this before, and I didn't really feel like sitting through another round of Teresa's snottiness right now. "Well, it's no big deal anyway, is it? I mean, Uncle Shoe'll be back with batteries any minute now. And if we get snowed in, who cares? It's *snow*, people. It's all the fun in the world and it's free."

"I've got people to talk to." Teresa grabbed the phone again, got up and began pacing while trying to get it to work.

My sister was a lost cause, but I knew that even Mark had to be a little bit excited. "It'll be totally cool," I told him. "What are you afraid of? Do you think we'll get snowed in and miss Christmas?"

He looked at me as if I insulted his intelligence. "Get a grip. There won't be enough to do that, blizzard or no blizzard."

"I don't know about that," Teresa said softly. She had stopped in front of the window.

Mark and I got up to look.

Deep, threatening clouds had replaced the bright morning sky, and it suddenly felt like the end of the day.

"Have you ever seen it get so dark, so fast?" Teresa whispered.

"It's definitely going to snow. Big time." Mark sized up the situation. He always looked at every problem like a broken radio. Lots of wires, but only one right way to connect them.

"You guys are worrying over nothing." I didn't see any reason to worry about it. We were safe. We had shelter. We had heat. Uncle Shoe would be coming back with all kinds of good grub. If we did get snowed in, we couldn't be any more set.

"Well, I haven't been sledding in a couple of years, and it'd be pretty cool to walk some of the mountain when it's covered in snow," my brother said.

It was a radical decision for Mark. He's a responsible, dependable guy. Doesn't get into trouble much. No sense of adventure. It might be the reason many people think he's boring. Teresa was right. He doesn't have many friends.

"How long's Uncle Shoe been gone?" Teresa placed her elbows on the window sill and lowered her head to rest on her hands.

"Not even thirty minutes," Mark replied, wiping his breath from the window.

I wanted a better look, so I walked over and opened the door.

A frigid, piercing breeze met me at the opening.

"YEOW!" I slammed the door before my face froze off. Even through my sweatshirt I felt that.

As I turned to grab my jacket, something hit the house.

It sounded like someone was on the roof. More than one person. Lots of them. Maybe even a hundred. And they were all tapping their fingers on the shingles.

I moved to the window, where Mark still sat staring moodily out at the mountain.

Teresa backed away from the window, looking at the ceiling. "What is it? What's it doing?"

Mark had his head as close as he could to the window, and was looking up in the sky. "I don't believe it. It's hailing."

"It's what?" I moved to the window.

"Hailing. Frozen water. Ice from the sky. And there's snow coming down with it."

I saw it then. Like tiny ice cubes.

"Can Uncle Shoe drive in this?" Teresa's voice sounded a little nervous.

"It's possible. But he might just pull over and let the storm run its course. Hail's like little rocks. With all of them coming down on your car while you're driving, it's easy to lose direction. He could go off the road or something."

Teresa gasped, and suddenly even I felt a little worried.

"But chill, you guys," Mark continued. "Uncle Shoe's not going to drive in this stuff. He'll be back as soon as it lets up."

It wasn't going to let up. The wind was already bending back the trees, and the snow and hail and whatever else came with it fell to the ground faster and harder.

The radio went silent, signaling that the power had been knocked out.

Just like that, the storm had arrived.

We weren't going anywhere.

"We'd better make sure everything's secure." Mark went over to the door and locked it. "It's a strong wind. It could blow a door open, or any of these windows out. Uncle Shoe's got a generator for the refrigerator in case something like this happens. I'll go turn it on and check all the windows on this floor. You guys go check upstairs."

I'd never been in a storm like this before, but it couldn't be all that bad. Still, if it would ease Mark's mind and keep him from bugging me all night, I'd personally glue every window shut.

On my way up, I passed the fireplace and noticed it was empty.

"The fire's gone out. Do we have anymore paper to help re-light the wood?"

"Uncle Shoe has some newspapers in the

basement. Go grab a few. Teresa, you take care of the windows upstairs."

"All right, all right! Don't be so bossy!" The wind and hail had made my sister nervous; her hands were shaking and her eyes grew wider with every word she spoke.

"We've got to be prepared. There are a hundred things that could happen in a bad storm like this." Mark seemed a little on edge, too.

As I jerked open the basement door and jumped the bottom stairs to the ground, I began to get that action rush. It was that feeling of beating the odds; that superhero feeling.

What I saw in the basement jolted me out of my dream world.

Did Mark say *some* newspapers?

From one wall to the other, the entire room was practically filled with stacks and stacks of old newspapers. There was enough light left outside to beam weakly through the basement window and show me the hidden morgue. The whole room suffered from the moldy smell of years of neglect.

"Fire hazard," I mumbled as I grabbed a few of the papers closest to the door. Then I noticed the stack in the corner. They looked new, whiter than the rest. I looked through the plastic wrapping at the cover of the first one.

"TRACKING BIGFOOT"
30 Man Expedition Sets Out
to Prove Sasquatch is Real.

"MAX? WHERE ARE YOU?"
"COMING!"

Why did Uncle Shoe keep so many papers, and why did he take such special care of these? *Well, hermits do what hermits do*, I thought.

I met Teresa coming down from upstairs as I came through the basement door. Mark was in the den lighting one of the lanterns my uncle kept. He placed it by the window.

"Where do you think he is?" Teresa walked to the window and looked out into the white downfall.

"Bad weather. He's probably driving slow," Mark said in a very unconvincing tone.

Sitting down on the floor, I watched Mark and Teresa fidget at the windows for a few moments. If they kept at it, they would start to make *me* nervous.

I wished the radio worked. I'd just put it on a loud station and drown them out.

Then I remembered.

My Walkman!

It was still in my bag. I hadn't listened to it in the last couple of days.

I marched into the bedroom to retrieve it. Grabbing it from my backpack, I ripped off its battery door to see.

"Oh, man . . ."

They were gone. My batteries were gone.

"Teresa . . ."

She had probably borrowed them and shoved them in the phone charger at some point, and now they were dead, too.

"Perfect," I muttered.

I decided to relax, so I lay back on the bed and listened to the hail hit the roof. It had quite a soothing effect, but I decided not to tell my brother and sister about it. Before I knew it, I was dozing in and out of sleep. I must have been like that for quite awhile. When the bad weather woke me up, I returned to the den where they informed me that Uncle Shoe had been gone two hours. By car, it's supposed to take about fifteen minutes at most, down the mountain. Another ten to town.

The snow pounded against the house, making it hard to see anything outside. And it had grown even darker. Mark turned up the lantern to full blast because, in spite of what the clock said, it looked like nighttime. He placed it on the table beside me, then began picking up the mess he'd made earlier.

Teresa sighed and walked away from the window, hopped on the couch, picked up the phone and tried again for a dial tone.

I continued to gaze outside, hoping to see headlights pull up the drive. The snow was smacking the window in waves, leaving it sort of clear for a few seconds at a time. It didn't take me long to learn the timing.

Snow.

Clear.

Nothing.

Snow.

Clear.

Nothing.

Snow, Clear, Something. *Something!* Something moved outside. In the front. At the edge of the trees.

"Uncle Shoe?"

Suddenly, the window next to me shattered violently, sending the lantern to the floor.

Flames crackled to life at my feet.

"FIRE!"

I think everyone yelled at the same time.

The lantern's flame jumped onto the rug under me and started a quick blaze.

"MAX, GET OUT OF THE WAY!" Mark leaped over the couch and started batting out the fire with a large pillow from the couch.

Then I felt the heat on my leg.

"AAAGGGGHHHH! MY PANTS LEG!"

Mark was up again. He beat my leg furiously with the pillow.

"ARE YOU OKAY?"

"YEAH!"

We both suddenly realized we were screaming at each other. We collapsed on the floor in the dark. We were just beginning to catch our breaths when the cabin was suddenly filled with light.

"WHAT NOW?" I yelled.

"Lantern number two." Teresa had found one of the other lamps and lit it. She walked towards us, but stopped and gasped when she saw something on the other side of the couch.

"WHAT? WHAT IS IT?" I was yelling every sentence now.

Teresa bent down slowly, and came back up with the cell phone.

It was crushed.

"Oh. Oh, man . . ." Mark lowered his face into his hands. "I thought I heard something crunch under me when I jumped up."

Sure enough, I saw the Fairfield Cellular label hanging from the bottom of his boot.

"We couldn't have used it anyway." I turned accusingly toward my sister. "But we might have been able to if Teresa hadn't swiped my Walkman batteries and used them up."

"What are you talking about, gnome? I never took your batteries!"

"Well, someone did. I put new ones in the other day when we pulled up into the driveway.

I put the dead ones in my pocket and the new ones in my . . . uh, oh." I reached slowly into my coat pocket. There should've been two dead batteries in there. One, two . . . three, four.

The groans that filled the room when I pulled them all out of my pocket were painfully long and loud.

"You had good batteries the whole time. Great, Max, just great." Teresa loved it when she was innocent.

"Wait. This may be okay. If I can get the phone working, we can still use those batteries to charge it. Give them to me." Mark snatched them from me, grabbed the phone from Teresa, and set up his workshop in the middle of the floor.

"What about the window, genius?" Teresa never liked having any telephone taken from her.

"There's got to be something around here to cover it. Max, help her find something."

Any other time I might have snapped at Mark by now for telling us what to do. But he'd just saved my life. He hadn't paid me that much attention in years. I'd let him slide this time.

"I saw some kind of model thing upstairs. We can use the wood under it to cover the window," Teresa said. Then she lit a third lantern and led me upstairs.

It was the first look I'd had at Uncle Shoe's room because the door was usually closed. He kept it nice and tidy. The bed was made, the books were all straight on their shelves, and the model we were looking for was set up neatly in the corner.

Teresa held the lantern only inches from it, revealing small models of a range of mountains. All of them had tiny red flags placed at certain spots, and the different ranges were labeled; Himalayans, Andes, and even Crier Mountain with one flag in it.

She repositioned the light so she could see me. "This will definitely cover that window, don't you think? The snow'll never get through."

"Teresa, I think I saw something outside."

Her face grew puzzled. "What?"

"I'm not sure. Something moving."

"It was probably a tree."

"It wasn't that big."

"Maybe it was a small tree."

"Maybe."

"Let's get that window boarded up," she said, and anxiously tipped the paper maché mountains onto the bed.

Our window repair job couldn't have been more of a pain.

Mark wouldn't let us do the job on our own. He had to supervise the whole thing, and by the time it was over, I wanted to throw my brother out into the snow.

"Well, if you're going to do it, do it right. Don't be slack about it," my brother said. "Besides if you don't seal it up tight, we'll freeze."

"I wish Uncle Shoe was here," I said. "At least then we'd be taking orders from someone with a clue."

I could see the tension building in Mark's red face. Then Teresa hammered in the last nail to seal the window.

"I've got an idea," she said. "How about you two make a fire and I'll sit and argue with myself." My sister had a way of shutting us up and moving us on.

As I crumpled up papers and Mark filled the fireplace with them, Teresa staked claim to the couch.

"You know, this is a blizzard," she said.

"Uh, yeah . . ." my brother answered.

"Well, didn't anybody know this thing was coming? I mean, the weatherman himself figured it out just a short time before it hit. Can't they usually spot these storms in advance? Especially one this big?" Teresa had really thought this out.

"Teresa, you can't predict the weather. Scientists can spend all the money they want to on it and weathermen can make their predictions for the next day, but in the end, no one knows for sure. All they can do is gather up percentages and possibilities," Mark explained.

"Gee, Mark, that's interesting. Now could you stuff more paper into the fireplace?" I asked. I couldn't help bringing him back down to earth, and once I'd said it, he hit me in the head with a wadded up newspaper.

"It's just weird is all," Teresa trailed off, then lay back and pulled the blanket over herself.

Mark took a candle from one of the tables, lit it with the lantern's flame, and held it into the fireplace. Within seconds we had a cozy fire.

Plopping in the chair with one of the many comic books I'd brought with me, I noticed Teresa was already asleep. I watched Mark return to his workshop on the floor. He picked up the pieces of the phone, and studied them one by one.

I started feeling bad about how I treated him earlier. He'd stopped the fire from burning off my leg and now he was going to sit up and work on the phone so that we might all be saved. I suppose I was mad at him for being so uptight and commanding. I knew if I told him about what I thought I saw outside, he'd just explain it away as something dull and boring.

He set the pieces down on the floor and rubbed his eyes.

"Do you think you can fix it?" I whispered.

"I'm pretty sure I can," he said. "I've never messed with one of these before, but it doesn't look too hard."

Teresa tossed a little in her sleep, and I glanced over to see if she had woken up. She hadn't.

"This whole thing has her spooked pretty bad," I said.

"It's her paranoid nature. She always thinks someone's talking about her. That's why she's on the phone all the time."

"But aren't you a little paranoid about the snow, too?" I asked him.

"I'm not paranoid. I'm just cautious. But now that everything's settled, I can relax like you," he said.

"I'm relaxed?" I didn't understand.

"Well, I'm always taking steps to make sure bad things don't happen, but you always need proof that something's wrong. That's where we're different, I guess," Mark explained. I had to really think about it, but he was right.

My mind flashed to a blurred image of *whatever it was* moving around outside.

"Yeah. I always need proof," I said.

It could've been a tree. It could've been a bird. It could've been anything. I just didn't know for sure.

I don't remember falling asleep.

I'm not even sure what it was that woke me up.

The house was very quiet.

I'd passed out in the chair. Teresa was on the couch, and Mark lay on the floor beside the scattered phone. They were still asleep.

I got up quietly to have a look around. Uncle Shoe had to be there.

Maybe in the kitchen.

I figured he probably came in early that morning, since the weather had been so bad during the night. He saw us asleep, and decided to make breakfast for us. It sounded good, anyway.

The kitchen was empty. A few drops from the faucet let me know we still had water. We'd left it dripping like Uncle Shoe always did, so the pipes wouldn't freeze.

As I passed the fridge on my way to the sink, my stomach growled to life. Breakfast. I opened the door to see what I could make myself. Cheese. Three slices of American Singles, all that were left from a pack of sixteen. Just enough for the three of us. I took mine out and decided I needed more light to eat by.

When I opened the shades, I almost went blind. My eyes weren't prepared for something that bright. Everything was covered with snow, and the stuff was still coming down! It fell lightly, adding a whiter layer on what already seemed too white.

It was a sledding dream.

Breakfast forgotten, I moved through the house, silently collecting everything I needed for a ride down the slopes.

It only took one glance at that snowy heaven to make me forget all the scary things that'd happened the day and night before. If I was going to be stuck in this trap, I wasn't going to suffer. This would probably be my best chance to shoot the hills.

My only problem? Mark had his feet propped up on old Thunder Blades. Well, he could have it. The old thing didn't really look safe anyway. I'd use my big, yellow doughnut.

Sliding the latch on the door as quietly as I could, I opened it slightly and slipped out.

There is nothing like walking on the snow. You're surrounded by the same color everywhere you look, and it's like exploring another world. The cold air wakes up your brain. It tells you to *jump in this white stuff, boy, and make a mess of yourself.*

That's exactly what I had to do.

The forbidden slope, The Cut, was mine.

I remembered where Uncle Shoe said it was. Just through the woods to the right of his house, the rockiest slope in sight.

It looked dangerous enough.

The slope looked for all the world like a long, bumpy white tongue that led to an open, grinning mouth at the bottom of the hill. There were boulders at every turn. The Cut probably meant the ten foot wide gorge at the bottom of the ride. That's where it was the most dangerous. Either you had enough speed, or you didn't. Once you started, there wasn't any chickening out.

I hated pulling a stunt like this with no one there to see, but Mr. Mark Responsible would never let me do it. And if Teresa knew, she'd just tell Mark. I had to go ahead and do it while the snow was there, with no one around to stop me. Who knew if I'd ever get another chance?

It took me five minutes to inflate my inner tube with my foot pump. Another five to stare down the chute from the top of the hill.

"It would be a terrible tragedy for me to discolor this wonderful white blanket of pure snow with my horrible, nasty red blood."

I looked up to see if anyone was listening.

Then I stared back down the hill.

You always wanted to make The Cut . . .

Uncle Shoe's words echoed in my head and I started imagining things at the bottom of the hill. One by one, the twisted, mangled bodies of the kids who had taken on The Cut appeared. They all lay in the snow on the other side of the gorge, moaning in pain as if they called out to their own personal Florence Nightingales. They continued to pile up. There had to be hundreds of them. No one walked away unscarred.

Suddenly I didn't want to go sledding.

I backed away from the hill, and stepped on the edge of my foot pump. It sprang up and struck me in the calf, which made me spin around so quickly that I lost my balance and fell back into my inner tube.

And it started moving.

By the time I got turned around, it was too late.

I was shooting The Cut.

Passing the first four boulders with increasing speed, I knew it would be the seventh or eighth rocks that would tell the tale. My speed there had to be good. And it was.

But it was the tenth turn that got me.

The front of my tube crashed into a rock at full force, flipping it over and sending me into the air and down the hill, tubeless.

I felt like a pinball as I bounced to and fro, unable to slow myself, until finally getting my feet in front of me and burying my heels deep into the snow.

I stopped myself inches away from the gorge.

My heart raced. I couldn't catch my breath. I must have sounded like a tired dog, breathing like I was.

"I . . . I . . . I am so stupid sometimes."

I lay there for another ten minutes or so, scared to death. Then I got up to look for my tube.

It had landed on the other side of the gorge.

"Stupid, yellow doughnut!" I shouted. "Big, yellow traitor!"

I turned away disgustedly, and slowly huffed my way back over the top the hill, not really looking ahead, just keeping my eyes on the ground.

Even though I was aching from hitting the rocks, and my tube was gone, I couldn't stay in a bad mood with so much snow around.

I couldn't help humming *Let It Snow*.

I stuck out my tongue to try to catch some of the white stuff as it fell.

Mountain snow tasted better than city snow, that's what I was thinking when I stepped into it. When my body froze and I knew I'd been right.

I stood in front of my uncle's house, right at the edge of the trees.

And I was looking at my foot.

It was dwarfed, standing in the center of another footprint.

The footprint of something smaller than a tree, but still very, very big.

9

I ran into the house and slammed the door behind me.

"MAX, WHAT'S WRONG WITH YOU?!" Teresa yelled, sitting bolt upright.

"THERE'S SOMETHING OUT THERE! I TOLD YOU LAST NIGHT THERE'S SOME-THING OUT THERE AND I WAS RIGHT! THERE'S SOMETHING OUT THERE!"

"You didn't say anything like that last night." Mark was still groggy, rubbing his eyes, and trying to wake up.

"He did to me. What'd you see, Max?" Teresa sounded like she almost believed me.

"FOOTPRINTS! I SAW BIG FOOTPRINTS!"

"IT MUST BE UNCLE SHOE! HE'S BACK!" Mark hopped to his feet and looked for the truck

38

outside. "Maybe he's parked out back. I'll go look!"

"NO. NOT UNCLE SHOE! IT'S NOT UNCLE SHOE. IT'S SOMETHING ELSE. IT'S BIGGER!"

I stopped screaming for a second and caught my breath. They weren't going to understand unless they saw it for themselves. "It's right out here in the front. Come look for yourselves. But let's leave this door open and be ready to run at any second, okay?"

"Let's just go see it, Max," Teresa said softly.

Both of them grabbed their coats and let me lead the way out into the snow.

I knew what was there, but I tried to gauge their reactions. Wondering whether they believed me or not was driving me crazy.

"There." I pointed.

"That? That's a bear track," Mark said.

"No way. There's no bear with a foot like that. It's huge. And it has six toes," I argued.

"It's a stupid bear track that's melted. That makes it look larger."

"I don't think that's a bear track, Mark," Teresa finally said.

Not even a second afterwards, we heard the growl. It came from the woods in front of us.

"What the . . .?" Mark stepped back.

It came again. A horrible, tortured growl that seemed to be coming closer.

"LET'S GO!" Mark turned and led the charge back inside the house.

He slammed the door and I locked it as Teresa jumped behind the couch.

"NOW DO YOU BELIEVE ME? HAVE YOU EVER HEARD A BEAR THAT SOUNDED LIKE THAT?" I yelled at Mark as I peered out the window.

Mark just stood there, staring at the locked door.

Teresa poked her head up from behind the couch. "That was no bear," she said. Then we all heard the growl again.

10

The noises didn't stop.

I ran down to the basement and grabbed the stack of newspapers I'd seen the night before. When I came back up, I found Mark pacing from window to window, and he'd barricaded the door.

"A bear could break down the door, but it'll never get in through these windows. They're way too small," Mark said.

"Are you crazy? That's not a bear track!" Teresa insisted. I thought she'd acted paranoid before, but now it started kicking into high gear. Since we ran back into the house, she hadn't moved from her spot behind the couch.

I dropped the papers to the floor and grabbed Mark's screwdriver to rip open the wrapping.

"Come here. Check this out."

Teresa moved to the floor and picked through the first couple of newspapers.

Mark reluctantly stepped away from the window to check out the pile. He looked at the first headline on the stack.

"You're nuts. There isn't a Bigfoot outside," he said.

"How do you know, Mark?" I couldn't stand the way he was always so sure of what he thought, and how other people's ideas didn't mean anything. Any sympathy I'd had for him the night before was now thrown out the window.

"Max, how much do you know about Bigfoot?"

"He's a big monkey-man who runs through the woods. Like an ape, but taller. And fatter."

"Don't you think if we had a Bigfoot in these woods, someone would've seen it by now?"

"Then tell me this, Mark. Why does Uncle Shoe have all of these newspapers separated from the rest, and the one thing they have in common are their Bigfoot stories? He knows something is in these woods!"

"Did you ever think he just might be an enthusiast? Someone who just likes to read about the legend of Bigfoot? And call it

Sasquatch. Bigfoot sounds so stupid!"

"He isn't just an enthusiast. He's got models. He's got models upstairs of all kinds of mountain ranges. And they've all got flags in them, Mark. One of those models was this mountain! I bet that's where the Big . . . the Sasquatches have been sighted. I'll bet you my *Walkman* on it."

"Max, hundreds and hundreds of people come to this mountain every year. There's never been a sighting, or it would've been all over town. If something like that were on this mountain, it'd be found."

"Max is right, Mark," Teresa said. She'd been completely silent up until then, sitting in a ball next to the couch. "You keep to yourself. You don't know. And Max is always too busy getting into trouble to listen to anybody. But I talk to people everyday. Call it gabbing if you want, but I talk to people all over town. And you wanna know what I'm hearing? There's something strange happening around Fairfield. Weird things are going on all the time, and no one seems to know why. I didn't believe it myself until I saw that footprint, but now I know that we're in it now, too. And whatever is out there, it isn't a bear."

11

"Maybe Uncle Shoe had an accident."

They were the first words Mark had spoken in twenty minutes.

He and I sat at opposite windows so we could see the front and the back of the house.

Teresa had opened one of the many cans of beans in Uncle Shoe's cupboard, and shoveled them into her mouth without any sign of chewing. She still sat on the couch.

"The roads may have been slick when he left. His truck could've skidded and he could've gone off the road," Mark continued.

I listened but didn't say anything. I kept my eyes focused on the spot where I found the footprint. Maybe Bigfoot creatures crossed back over their own tracks.

"You're being pretty morbid, Mark," Teresa answered him.

"It would explain why he never returned. He may be in the hospital, unconscious or something."

It dawned on me that the snow was still falling. Lightly, but it still fell. I'd never seen so much snow in my life. The track I'd seen was probably covered by now. If the Bigfoot, or Sasquatch, or whatever, disappeared, the only evidence we had of the thing existing was now gone.

"But what about Mom and Dad? They have to know we're in trouble!" Teresa snapped. Just then I saw a branch move just a few feet from the footprint.

"I thought about that yesterday, December 10th," Mark answered.

I watched the limb bounce up and down.

"December 10th? Their anniversary! It was their anniversary and we all forgot it!"

Something was coming through the brush.

"I bet Dad didn't forget. I bet he took Mom somewhere nice for the weekend. Dumped us off here."

An arm moved the branch again. It came out so suddenly I didn't think it was real. But then it sunk in. An arm. A white arm. A white, hairy arm. With claws.

"No wonder they wanted us to stay with Uncle Shoe! We were totally had!"

Then it looked me square in the eyes with its glowing, red stare and howled. A blackened face surrounded by snow white fur.

"If I'm right they'll be getting back today. If I'm right . . ."

When it showed its teeth, I finally screamed.

"THERE! I SEE IT! I SEE IT! THE SASQUATCH!"

Mark and Teresa were way too slow to see it come out of the trees, but they still saw enough.

The monster strode into the front yard, and across the driveway up near the porch.

It must have been about seven feet tall. Thinner than I thought it would be. Its white hair was longer, and definitely unwashed since it knotted at the ends. The creature took long strides, swinging its arms back and forth like it had big rocks tied to its hands.

It looked at us once.

And then again.

The face looked human. But it wasn't. Those eyes. They glowed. How could that be?

It disappeared into the trees on the other side of the yard, and let out that scream that sounded like a horn.

Everything inside moved with a blur.

Mark ran into the kitchen, and I heard something crash to the floor.

Teresa started to whimper out the first bits of a full fledged bawl.

I looked from her, then back out the window.

Was it coming back?

Where was it?

Something rammed into the door to the kitchen and I saw a table trying to squeeze its way through. Mark grunted from the other side, and pushed. The legs came off one by one as he shoved it through.

"HOW MANY OF THEM ARE OUT THERE?"

"ONE. I ONLY SAW ONE!"

The table fell to the floor.

"It's got two halves and a middle leaf. That's three windows we can cover! I'll get the long nails. Teresa, go pull all the drapes so that thing can't see us!

"I'M NOT PULLING THE DRAPES. YOU PULL THE DRAPES!"

"TERESA, DO IT! JUST DO IT!"

"NO!"

I pulled the drapes. I pulled every one in the house because I wanted to see that thing again. It was better if I saw it, because then I knew where it was. I didn't like not knowing.

But it wasn't there.

I looked out every window and didn't see it. I finished with the last window upstairs when Mark rushed in the room.

"That's not enough . . ."

He grabbed Uncle Shoe's dresser and pushed it over to the window, covering about half of it.

The other window needed something to block it, too.

"How about the bed? Let's block the other one with the bed!" My brain finally started to kick in and think again.

"Yeah . . ."

We heaved the mattress onto the floor and lifted the box springs to cover the second bedroom window.

"Any others?" Mark asked.

"You've covered everything downstairs?"

"Everything."

"So it can't get in?"

Mark didn't say anything.

We both slouched to the floor to catch our breaths, listening to Teresa sob downstairs.

Trouble came about an hour later.

Teresa had settled down with a cup of Ramen noodles Mark had made for her before he constructed himself a cheese sandwich with his slice of the American Singles.

My spoon hit the bottom of my can of beans.

"What do you think they eat?" I asked anyone who wanted to answer.

"I've read a few things about the Sasquatch, if that's what it is. They're supposed to eat berries, leaves, bugs, stuff like that." Mark stared at the broken cell phone as he talked, like he was trying to fix it in his head.

"Did you ever read anything about glowing, red eyes? I've never heard of any animal having glowing, red eyes." I tried to snap him out of it.

It worked. He looked right at me.

"Nope."

"What if . . . what if one of those things got Uncle Shoe?" Teresa had stopped sipping her noodle soup and returned her attention to the conversation.

I couldn't answer and neither could Mark, but it made me think.

Uncle Shoe had Sasquatch on the brain, I was pretty sure of that. Why else would he have a stack of papers about the thing? And what about the models? Did he know the monsters were in these woods? Was he prepared for it?

"I'm going upstairs to check something out."

"Probably not a good idea," Mark said.

"If that thing came in here, we would have heard it. I'll be right back."

"No. Max stay here," Teresa begged.

I picked up the closest weapon.

"I'll take this hammer, okay? I'll be right back."

I peered up the stairs. It'd gotten darker in the last hour. I got my hammer ready to strike and walked up slowly, like I'd seen in a hundred action films where the hero invades the evil fortress.

It had gotten really cold at the top of the stairs, but that was okay. It kept me alert. I made my way into Uncle Shoe's room.

The models lay scattered on the bed where Teresa had dumped them the night before. But I wasn't interested in them. I wanted to see the books.

My uncle had a good many on his shelves. Everything from Mark Twain classics to Arthur C. Clarke.

But there was one section, the entire second shelf, devoted to the mystery of Sasquatch.

I pulled them all off the shelf and started looking at the covers. I stopped at one.

ABOMINABLE SNOWMEN
by Ivan T. Sanderson

The illustration of the creature on the front of the book was the closest thing I could find to what was walking around outside.

Abominable Snowmen. Yetis. I'd heard of them. They're like Bigfoot, but they hang out in the snow. But I thought they lived in larger, colder areas, like the Himalayas or somewhere up in Canada.

What were they doing here?

I flipped through the book some more but I couldn't find any mention of red eyes anywhere.

What were these things?

There were other books, even some on Fairfield history. I grabbed up a few to take downstairs. That's when it started.

The thumping.

The scratching.

The screaming.

The thing was attacking the house from outside.

Instantly, Teresa began screaming and I ran down the stairs, taking the bottom half in a single leap.

Mark had grabbed a spare piece of wood and we moved back to back into the middle of the den, watching the walls shake around us.

Pictures fell to the floor and the window glass rattled in its frame.

The screams grew louder.

The whole house must have been surrounded.

"HOW MANY OF THEM ARE THERE?!" Mark yelled.

Definitely more than one. There had to be. The pummeling came from every direction.

Teresa screamed again, like she'd had enough, then scooped up Mark's screwdriver.

"GET OUT OF HERE! LEAVE US ALONE!" she yelled.

BAM!

The loudest blow yet.

They wanted in.

They wanted us.

That's when I flipped.

Screaming at the top of my lungs, I ran to the spot the blow had come from and smashed it with the hammer.

Then I hit it again. And again, hollering all the while.

The wood was so thick that a hammer didn't do much damage, but I kept slamming it into the wall anyway.

I didn't quit until Mark finally grabbed my wrist.

"It's cool," he said. "They've stopped."

"Yeah, yeah." I tried to catch my breath. "But Mark, I think they want more than leaves and berries."

"Now let's divvy these up," Teresa command-
ed. She sat down beside her pile of household
weapons that she had taken twenty minutes to
rummage up.

There were Uncle Shoe's cutting knives,
three flares, an old baseball bat, an ice pick, a
set of rusted golf clubs, various pieces of wood,
and lots of tiny objects good for throwing.

Teresa knew we'd have to fight our way out
of there. Unlike Mark, who still worked diligent-
ly to fix the phone, my sister had accepted the
fact that no one was coming to help us. It was
totally unlike her to lead the pack like this, but
fear does strange things to people.

"I'd guess there were ten of them. With all
that banging, there would have to be at least

that many," she said, grabbing the knives for herself.

"Teresa, forget that stuff," Mark told her. "If those things get in here, you're not going to have time to defend yourself. They'll be all over you in a second."

"Well, what are you going to do, Mark? Call 9-1-1 and tell them we have yetis? The phone doesn't even work!" Teresa was frustrated, and wanted action. The time for talk was over for her and she wanted to get out of there any way she could.

I flipped through the books, trying to find anything that could help us.

"People have been seeing these things since about 1906 all around the world, but mostly in Asia. It says one guy even managed to catch one, but it escaped later."

"Who cares? How do you kill them?" Teresa asked.

"Same as any animal, I guess. Most of these guys go hunting for them with guns though, not steak knives."

"What're we going to do then? Sit here and wait for them to come in?"

"Well, Teresa," Mark said with a sly grin crossing his face. "I guess we call 9-1-1."

He held up the phone. The green "ON" light was flashing. Mark had done it. He'd fixed the phone.

"ALL RIGHT!" Teresa and I cheered.

"I put the batteries in the charger and the phone in the cradle and there you go. It'll take about an hour to power up, and then let's just pray the weather's clear enough to get a call through."

Mark and I high-fived, but Teresa held back. She heard the scratching first.

She shushed us frantically. We sat in a circle on the floor, trying to pin down exactly where it was coming from.

15

Mark turned up the lantern's flame.

We each panned around the room, searching for the noise's source.

I imagined the claws of one of the larger ones digging its way through the house. Imagining the thing getting a good grip on the inside wood and ripping away the entire wall sent me into sweat. Is that what they were trying to do?

I found myself standing up and holding the bat Teresa had dropped on the floor. She stood next, scanning in a different direction. Mark looked up the stairs, listening to hear if the scratching came from there.

No one could tell.

Mark eased up the steps until he finally disappeared into the dark. I listened for a scream. I just knew he would scream.

"Bring up that other lantern and help me check the rooms," he whispered to Teresa from the top floor.

"Can't you tell where it's coming from?" my sister softly asked back.

"No, but I definitely think the scratching is coming from up here somewhere!"

Teresa grabbed one of the lanterns and went to meet him at the top of the stairs. With that light gone, it felt as if half of the sun left the room. Even though my brother and sister were just a few feet away, I felt alone in the dark.

Like a moth to a flame, I descended on the other lamp. The very second I scooped it off the ottoman, I saw the light at the top of the stairs disappear around the corner.

Someone has to keep an eye out down here, I told myself. That was the only logic I could muster up at the moment, but it kept me down there alone.

"WHAT IS IT?" I yelled, turning the flame in the lantern down instead of up. A total acci-dent, but Mark defused the scare by giving me good news.

"It's a tree limb scratching this window! Stop yelling! We're going to check the others now."

"Sorry. Just concerned," I answered, and then felt something tap slightly against my foot.

Water. A clear stream of it had washed out of the kitchen. It crept across the floor and into the den.

What spilled?

Had the pipes frozen? Burst maybe?

Looking in the kitchen I saw the water coming from under the refrigerator. What was leaking from there?

I stepped in, this time making sure I correctly adjusted the lantern's flame so I could see the whole room.

Nothing jumped out at me. The windows were all boarded up. Everything looked cool, except for the water pouring from the fridge. And something else . . .

Less noise. The kitchen was usually louder. Why?

The generator. That was it. The little generator that kept the refrigerator running must've gone out, letting the freezer ice melt and run out.

Uncle Shoe kept the little power pumper in a utility closet right beside the fridge.

Maybe Mark can fix it, I thought.

Just as I grabbed the knob and pulled the closet door open, I heard something on the other side.

Scratching?

16

Reaching with its clawed paw through a hole in the back of the closet, a screaming yeti gripped my shirttail and yanked me towards itself.

My butt hit the floor, hard.

I planted a foot on each side of the opening and tried to push away.

It yanked me again, but I held my place.

When I saw its head emerge from the opening I knew it had used me to pull its way through. It snarled, and its spit dotted my face.

There was something burning my hand!

THE LANTERN!

I still held on to it. Now it pressed against my knuckles and seared the skin covering them.

Swinging it over my head, I slammed the

lamp into the monster's arm. A fireball exploded out as the lamp shattered; leaving both of us screaming.

It let me go and I crawled back against the wall.

The opening looked like a 3D television to me, and I watched the yeti howl in pain because its arm and head were on fire. The monster backed out of the hole, and ran off into the snow.

My heart was pumping so hard I knew it'd be hours before it slowed down.

Mark and Teresa ran into the room and instantly saw the problem. My sister reached under my arms and dragged me out of the room while Mark grabbed a hammer and nails and sealed the closet and kitchen doors shut.

"MAX ARE YOU OKAY? MAX?" Teresa shook me.

It took me a second. "Yeah."

Mark popped into the room.

"Is he okay?"

"Yeah," said Teresa.

"Yeah," I repeated.

"How many did you see?"

"Just one."

"There have to be more of them than that.

They're probably trying to dig their way through all parts of the house."

Suddenly every piece of wood that held the house together creaked in unison. It sounded as if the whole place was about to come down.

"They aren't attacking. This is something else," Mark held his hands out to settle us down.

I thought the same thing. Not even the yetis could make the whole house creak like that.

With only one lantern now, the entire house took on a shadowy, foreboding feel, like it was turning against us, too.

Teresa grabbed the phone.

"It hasn't had time to charge yet," Mark told her.

She flipped the button a couple of times, and then smacked it against her palm, and listened . . .

"IT'S WORKING!"

"CALL 9-1-1!"

Teresa dialed the numbers at the speed of light and paced the room frantically while she waited for an answer. Mark bounced in his spot with anticipation.

I couldn't get enthused. My brother and sister hadn't seen the monster close up. A yeti grabbed me, I kept telling myself. I was still wiping its drool from my face.

The thing was vicious. If there were more of them, what chance did any rescue team have?

"I'VE GOT 'EM! I'VE GOT 'EM! HELP! WE NEED HELP!" Teresa went on to tell them our predicament. She stayed sharp, and told them we were surrounded by bears instead of yetis. They would've thought it was a prank and might not have shown up at all. The operator talked to her for a minute or two, then the signal started to fade. They broke up a few seconds after that.

It didn't matter. Teresa heard enough. "They've been rescuing people from the mountain all day. We weren't the only ones to get stuck. The weather's been so bad that they haven't been able to get up here yet, but they're hoping the storm will break soon, then they're going to send a helicopter up here."

Mark and I didn't have time to react at all

before the boards in the house groaned in protest against the incredible force from outside.

"It's the storm," Mark said. "It's getting worse."

The lantern's light seemed to dim even more.

When the blizzard winds met the house at their blustering worst, Mark never knew what hit him.

The board Teresa and I had slapped on the open window so haphazardly the night before blew from the wall and rocketed through the air. It struck my brother in the head and sent him instantly to the floor.

As I ran over to him, out of the corner of my eye I saw something white follow the board into the house.

Snow.

Heavy, pounding snow.

Carried into the house by a wind strong enough to throw us all the way back home if it wanted.

Mark had a gash in his head so large it looked like another mouth. His eyes seemed to spin around in their sockets. Blacking out would be the final step, and that came shortly after.

Teresa screamed.

"He's not dead! He's still breathing!" But as soon as I said it, I knew that wasn't the reason she backed away from the window with that terrified expression on her face.

Nothing had ever scared me as much as what I saw when I turned around.

Through the blowing snow, I saw twenty red eyes. Maybe thirty, and they were just a few yards from the house. Beacons of death that milled about anxiously in the blinding storm . . . and then came closer . . .

"THE HAMMER! GIVE ME THE HAM-MER!" I yelled to my sister as I grabbed the board and replaced it over the open hole.

Teresa slapped the hammer into my hand, climbed under me and held the board to the wall. I plucked the nails from the floor, held the extras sideways in my mouth, and drove each one into the wall with three swift swings of the hammer.

Teresa gritted her teeth so tightly I thought she'd crush them into powder. She held the board just long enough for me to put the last nail into the wall.

"THEY'RE GOING TO BREAK THROUGH IT, MAX! THERE'S TOO MANY OF THEM! WE'LL NEVER MAKE THE HELICOPTER!" Teresa was close to losing it.

"Uncle Shoe says snow that blows strong doesn't blow long."

"Yeah, well this snow's been blowing for two

days," she yelled back.

"But never like this. It's gonna be over soon. I can feel it. We've just got to wait it out. Upstairs. Upstairs is the safest place." Since they were breaking through every window on the bottom floor, I figured the den and kitchen were no longer secure. I was hoping the yetis would have trouble climbing, and we'd be safer in a smaller room with only one door to barricade.

Teresa looked at Mark, who was spread across the floor like a big 'X'. "How do we get him up there?" she asked.

"We can pick him up, can't we?"

As we carried him toward the steps, I noticed Mark seemed a lot heavier then he looked. I almost snapped at Teresa "put a little effort into it," but after we got Mark to the first step, I realized there would be no way we could get him to the top.

"He's just too heavy. I bet we couldn't even get him halfway up the stairs."

"Well, he's not waking up. We need something to pull him."

The thumping had started again.

I heard wood cracking. Teresa was right.

The yetis would break through.

I pored over the room for something, anything, that would help get Mark up those stairs.

Then I saw something I'd forgotten about completely.

The sled.

"Go to Uncle Shoe's room. Grab some of his belts," I told my sister, as I ran to grab ol' Thunder Blades.

Just as my hand touched the rusty blade, a claw burst through the wood on the door.

I picked up the sled and darted for the stairs. "TERESA!"

She appeared the very next second, gripping a handful of tacky belts like they were dead snakes.

"Drop those. Grab this, and put it under him when I lift him up!" I gave her the sled and she knew instantly what I wanted to do.

With every bit of strength I had left, I pulled Mark up, and held him there for the longest seconds of my life. I heard something grunt to the left of me, and I saw the yeti busting away the wooden barrier and coming through the window.

"Okay," Teresa started to say, but I couldn't

wait for the rest of it. I dropped Mark and headed for the closest weapon, the old baseball bat.

I ran over and let the yeti have it right in the face.

Before it could howl, I crowned it on top of the head.

The third time I swung, it grabbed the bat from me and crawled all the way in.

19

I'd been in fights before. I never started them, but I never let people walk all over me either. A bully who calls himself Count Nefarious shot me with his pellet gun once. It hurt like crazy. But after the sting left, I throttled the guy. He suffered his first defeat at my hands, and after that, I had to endure harsh, disciplinary action from my parents. But Nefarious never bothered me again. Anyway, I knew how to handle myself in tough scrapes.

But I'd never come across a yeti before.

When that thing forced its way in, all sense left me. I was beyond screaming. Beyond running away.

It stood in front of me. Between me and the stairs.

"TERESA! GET UPSTAIRS! I CAN'T GET AWAY!"

"MAX . . . " she cried out a few times, but I finally heard the blades cut into the stairs, and Mark's feet bouncing off each step as she dragged him up.

The beast had to be almost seven feet tall. I'd committed its teeth to memory. Its gums dripped with so much saliva that they glistened.

I didn't look any higher than the mouth. I kept my eyes on the rest of it, looking for my chance to break away and shoot up the stairs.

Watching its arms and legs, I wondered if its bones had broken in different places all over. Elongated limbs hung from its frame like yard-sticks, bending at the joints so independently of each other the entire beast looked like it was made of rubber.

Then it swung the bat.

I dodged just in time. Barely.

It swung awkwardly, like it tried to mimic what it had seen me do. Judging by its second swing, it learned quickly. Closer, but it still missed me.

Another yeti poked its head through the

window, and I heard a familiar scratching at the generator cabinet behind me.

I'm not going to get out of this. These things are going to catch me. THEY'RE GOING TO EAT ME.

My feet hit something on the floor. The radio.

I picked it up and launched it right at the monster, and the corner of it struck the yeti in the forehead. It roared in pain and continued forward.

I backed away quickly, scrambling over the furniture in an attempt to put distance between us. All the while I was grabbing things to throw; a lamp, a clock, and even my beloved Walkman.

I nabbed the ice pick from Teresa's weapons pile.

Tossing my jacket at the beast as a distraction, I rolled across the floor and lodged the ice pick deep into the monster's ankle.

The yeti trumpeted its agony so loud I thought it would stop my heart. Then what felt like five sharp pencils grabbed my thigh and dug in as I tried to scoot away.

The bat! It dropped the bat!

I grabbed the pine and, like a hammer to a

nail, drove the ice pick in deeper.

The yeti howled and loosened its grip on my thigh.

Freed for a moment, I got to my feet, but the other yeti was already in, blocking the stairway.

I veered to the right, racing for the basement door. Pulling it open, I expected to see a room full of yetis.

No yetis.

I jumped in, locked it, and started grabbing armloads of newspapers to build a makeshift barricade against the door.

I just knew they would burst through before I could get the door blocked. But everything was silent for a few precious seconds and I completed my blockade's construction.

Then the monsters slammed their fists against the door.

I jumped back and held my breath.

BAM! They pounded again.

I backed up, moving to the other side of the room.

BAM!

And then that was it.

There was nothing else; no fists crashing

into the door; not even any roaring.

They just stopped.

I finally allowed myself to breathe.

It seemed okay, at least for the next few seconds.

With a clear view of the room, I sized up my situation. There was no other exit. If the monsters got in, there'd be no place to run.

It took me a minute to calm down.

My thigh stung like crazy. It had swelled, and now just had a thick soreness to it. Would I have to get shots for something like that? Who knew what diseases those things might carry? With the monsters still tearing through the house, I'd consider myself lucky to get out with only a swollen thigh.

I shouted Teresa's name but couldn't hear an answer.

I didn't want to think the worst.

Maybe she barricaded herself in time. Maybe Mark woke up and they both escaped. I couldn't think about that right now.

One thing was for certain, though. I was alone.

The basement looked darker than before. By the clock, it was still daylight outside, but none of that light reached the basement like before. Why? I figured it out quickly when I saw snow piled high outside in front of the puny, smudged basement window. A window too small to crawl through. Soon, night would fall and I'd be left totally in the dark.

If I lasted that long.

I could hear the monsters tearing the place apart upstairs. Every so often they pummeled the door, just to let me know they remembered. I'm sure if they focused their efforts, they could've been in that basement eating me in a matter of seconds.

But they didn't. *Why?*

What had happened?

For a few seconds, I felt relief. They weren't bursting through the door to get me. But then I felt nothing but a heavy sense of dread.

What were they doing?

Where were they?

Were they . . . planning?

Maybe they were vegetarians. Or, if not, maybe they just weren't hungry yet, full from another meal. I doubted that.

By flipping through even a few of the books upstairs, I knew that no one who'd ever encountered a yeti had gone through anything like this.

No one had ever been this close before.

Or maybe someone had and didn't live to tell the tale.

Those conclusions were hard for me to believe. No matter how elusive people say the yetis, or the sasquatch, or any of the wildmen are, how could you not find something as big as that? With a thirty man expedition, it shouldn't take longer than a month to find one of these things, especially with today's technology.

So where do they come from? Where do they hide? Under the earth? What if they were human, and changed into yetis like someone might change into a werewolf? Of course you'd have to believe in werewolves.

That was the one that almost had me going. Because if you accepted the lore, it definitely gave a reason for Uncle Shoe's disappearance.

Uncle Shoe's a yeti! I couldn't believe I thought the words. But instead of changing into a creature when the moon came out, he may transform when it snowed.

Hey, maybe I was on to something. Maybe he left the house because he knew he would change. When he did, he joined a pack of who knows how many people who also became yetis. Now animals in every sense of the word, they all hunted for prey. That would be us. When the snow stopped, maybe they'd all return to normal and there'd be no one left to blow the whistle on them because they would've eaten all of us.

That's why Uncle Shoe wasn't with us.

I got up to walk around. This was crazy! My mind was wandering in a thousand weird directions, and paranoia was clouding my thinking. Next I would suspect Mark or Teresa of bringing them here with some kind of curse.

I was trying to come up with any reason to explain the fact that I was trapped in the dark alone.

Making steps with some of the newspapers, I climbed up to look through the little window. If this whole thing had happened two years earlier, I might've been small enough to climb through it.

Then I noticed it slid open from the side. I

pulled the window free and snow fell inside to the floor.

I grabbed a wooden board leaning against the wall and knocked away all of the snow around the window until I could see daylight.

CRASH!

Something hit the ground, knocking the board out of my hand and sending me tumbling backwards into the basement.

When I didn't hear growls, or see any white fur or red eyes, I inched back toward the window to see what had fallen.

Thunder Blades.

It'd fallen from above.

Then I saw the mess.

Scattered outside around the house were Uncle Shoe's things. Pictures of the family, socks, the mountain models, and books littered a small area beside the house.

The items were being thrown down from upstairs.

Teresa. Mark.

21

Had the yetis gotten them?

Would they be the next things to be thrown from the window?

I couldn't be the only one left. I couldn't be. I had to find a way out of the basement. I had to get to my brother and sister.

Only seconds after I climbed down from the window, the thrashing about upstairs stopped.

Now they made a new kind of noise, a never-ending hum with just a ripple of a growl mixed in. Every one of them must have been doing it, and they were all in sync. Soon, their monotone sound turned into a harmony.

Singing? These things trash a house and now they're singing about it? Why? This was getting weirder by the minute.

The volume rose. The tone became increasingly harsh, even violent. A fight song? Were they about to attack?

Don't worry about them, I thought. *Keep looking for a way out.*

For the tenth time I scoured the room, searching for an exit that didn't exist.

A wall separated the basement into two sections. Both sides were filled with newspapers. It had no back door, no large windows, nothing. The grey, cement block walls made it feel like a prison. It had a concrete floor. I couldn't even dig my way out.

I'd figured out which room the sled and the other items were thrown from. Maybe Mark and Teresa were in there. They might have thrown the stuff out.

Opening the door and making a run for it seemed to be the only way to get to my brother and sister, or what was left of them.

Even though I feared the worst, I decided not to yell to them. The fact that I'd stayed quiet and the yetis hadn't attacked me counted for something.

But I was still trapped.

"It's hopeless," I said, falling back on a pile of

papers.

Then I stared hard at the ceiling.

Was that a heating duct I saw up there?

Maybe . . .

I hopped up and examined it closely in the dim light.

It was indeed a heating duct, and, unlike the window, was big enough for me to crawl through. Only a shiny, new looking grate covered it. Four screws held it in place. If I could get them out, I could climb out of there and get to Teresa and Mark.

It sounded good, anyway. Plus, as desperate as I was, I couldn't think of anything else. First, I needed a screwdriver. I remembered seeing Mark's lying on the floor upstairs. That one wouldn't do me any good.

Luckily, these were flathead screws. I could use a quarter to turn them. And I did. I had exactly thirty-five cents in my pocket. Eleven cents less and I would've had no tools at all.

Still, it went painfully slow.

Even though the screws were new, it took a lot of effort to move them. They'd been put in pretty tight. But eventually I got one to move.

The others came quickly after that first one.

Yanking off the grate and looking up into the duct, I saw that it turned just a couple of feet up. I'd have to pull myself up there and crawl out.

I just had to stack more newspapers up in order to reach it.

Then I heard something in the distance.

It sounded like a fan at first, but then I realized *it had to be the helicopter*.

I ran over to the window to look, and sure enough, coming over the trees about a mile away sped a red rescue helicopter.

We were saved!

The nightmare was about to end!

If we could only get to the chopper.

The monsters' song swelled to a crescendo. . .

And that's when I noticed the wind picking up outside, and the snow falling a little harder.

No way. I couldn't believe it.

It seemed like they were controlling the snow.

Had they created the storm?

Maybe now they wanted to create a new blizzard to bring down the helicopter and prevent our rescue.

I couldn't let that happen.

22

"HEY! HEY, I'M DOWN HERE! REMEMBER ME? COME ON AND GET ME NOW CAUSE I'M GETTING AWAY!"

They kept singing.

"LISTEN. I REALLY WANT TO BE EATEN WHILE I STILL HAVE A LITTLE MEAT LEFT ON ME, SO COME AND GET IT!"

They still kept singing.

"OH—OKAY. YOU GUYS WANT TO SING? WE'LL SING!"

I started making the most hideous noises I could think of. It's a sound that my friend Mitchell Garrison taught me as a way to annoy teachers when their backs were turned. It begins as a rooster imitation, but once you add the "kamma kamma kamma" before it and the "weeeeeeeeeee" after it, you've got something no one can stand, including yetis.

They stopped almost instantly.

I couldn't be sure if they quit just to quit, or if they were coming after me.

When a furry arm practically split the basement door in two, I knew they had heard me.

I bounced back down into the room, and ran to the window. The helicopter had almost reached the house.

As the yetis tried to rip their way in, I climbed the stack of papers to the heating duct. I hadn't piled enough papers on to help me get through the opening, so I had to jump.

I struggled up into the duct, and caught the edge of the turn with my fingertips.

There wasn't anywhere to put my feet to push myself up, so I had to pull.

It wasn't going to happen.

My arms gave out and I fell out of the duct, onto the newspapers below.

The yetis knocked away the last pieces of the door, and began kicking out the paper barricade I'd put up against the door.

Without missing a beat, I grabbed the closest stacks of paper I could find, piled them on top of the others, and climbed back up into the duct.

As the monsters flooded the room, I hopped up into the duct's first turn, and crawled further in.

I felt the papers underneath my feet get knocked away by the monsters, and I'm sure they tried to grab my feet but I moved way too fast.

Under me were the vibrations of the yetis' fists striking the ceiling, hoping to knock me down.

I had to creep out of that position. If I could get through a couple of turns of the duct, maybe I'd lose them or they would forget about me.

Of course my heart wanted to pound out of my chest, and breathing in those cramped quarters was difficult. I could feel the grime all around me and the dust inside tried to choke me every second.

I had to get out of there quickly.

The first turn I hit was an upwards one. I couldn't see, but my hands gave me directions. Spinning around to lie on my back, I pushed myself into the turn inch by inch. Then I used my feet and my knees to push myself up through the duct.

Finally, I came to another opening on the main floor of the house.

Peeking out, I found I was over the den, and man, was it trashed! The couch looked as if they had fed on it, and the wood from the tables and the art from the walls were scattered all over the floor.

But I didn't see any yetis.

I could hear them, though.

From different rooms, from outside, and from under me in the basement, the white-maned devils had whipped themselves into a shrieking frenzy.

The helicopter was just outside.

Once the pilot saw Abominable Snowmen with glowing red eyes running around the house, my guess was he wouldn't come in and search the place.

He'd never find me.

I would have to kick out the vent, and jump down into the den. From there, I'd run upstairs and flag down the chopper.

Some plan, huh?

A suicide run, and I knew it.

I positioned my feet against the grate, and then pounded it with hard stomps. It seemed to loosen a bit. I'd have to keep trying.

Then I heard Teresa call out my name.

"MAX! MAX, WHERE ARE YOU?!"

Straining my legs to push the grate all the way off the wall, I couldn't help but cry out.

"TERESA! DON'T LET THEM LEAVE ME! I'M COMING!"

It wouldn't budge.

Suddenly the vent was ripped off of the wall in front of me.

The yeti must've been close to the wall.

I never saw it, and I didn't stick around to get a better look.

As it threw the grate to the ground, I leaped out just over it, hit the floor, rolled to my feet, and tore upstairs.

I could hear the monster coming right behind me.

Making a hard right, I saw that the door to the room where the stuff had been thrown from was ripped open. When I crashed in, I saw Mark, apparently recovered, swinging a long piece of wood at two of the creatures that had broken through. Teresa crouched in the window opening. I saw a harness that had been lowered by the helicopter appear right behind her.

"MAX!" she screamed. "LOOK OUT!"

I dropped to the floor, and then looked up to see the yeti I'd burned earlier pull its claw from the wall.

"THE CLOSET, MAX! GET INTO THE CLOSET! LOCK IT FROM THE INSIDE!" Mark yelled to me. He was keeping the monsters at bay with the board, but he knew I was defenseless.

He didn't have to tell me twice.

Launching myself through the closet door, I grabbed the knob and pulled it closed. An instant later, I latched it shut.

A cord dangled from the closet's ceiling. Even though I knew the electricity was out, I pulled the cord without thinking. Instead of light, a door opened above me and a ladder dropped down.

The attic.

"MAX, CAN YOU HEAR ME? MAX, THEY'RE ALL OVER THE PLACE!" Mark sounded close to being insane. I heard someone in the helicopter talking to us over a loudspeaker, but I couldn't make out the words over all the growls from the monsters and screams from my brother and sister.

Just as I was about to answer, I heard Mark cry out *"NO!"* It seemed to echo through the entire house.

Then nothing.

"M-Mark?" I called.

Two massive fur covered hands burst through the wood and grabbed each side of the door.

In the blink of an eye I scaled the ladder to the attic, just as one of the beasts stripped the door from the hinges.

With the ladder's rope in my hand, I drew it up hard and fast, smacking the monster in the chin and slamming the attic door shut.

The highest level of the house had been almost completely unused, except for a couple of storage boxes in the corner. Light beamed in from the window at the far end.

I made my way over to the window, sizing it up to see if I could crawl out, so the helicopter could pick me up.

The window was definitely big enough for me to fit through, but I couldn't get it open.

I screamed at the top of my lungs, and saw

the helicopter hovering outside.

Teresa and Mark were inside.

They saw me and yelled up front to the pilot, and as the helicopter hovered backwards, something began to pull it down.

I could see the pilot struggling with the controls. He lifted the craft in the air a little but then it jerked to the side and I saw the problem.

Hanging from the landing skids, two yetis were trying to climb aboard.

I backed up, away from the window, not knowing if the chopper would crash through the house or not.

Mark kicked one of the things in the face and it dropped to the ground.

The other one clambered up to the front, and smashed its claw right through the helicopter's front windshield.

I could see the pilot panic and grab a gun from next to his seat. Still trying to hold his craft in the air, he fired at the monster.

It was a flare gun.

The shot blinded me at first, then I saw he'd missed.

The chopper spun around with the yeti still pounding on the front of it. Panicked, the pilot grabbed another flare and fired again.

Right towards my window!

Glass shattered everywhere in an explosion of pink light. I jumped behind the boxes for cover to avoid being cut to ribbons.

Looking back quickly, I saw the flaming yeti fall from the smoking helicopter.

The rescue chopper veered to the right. I could only assume the pilot wanted to get some space between it and the house.

It kept getting lower and lower. I saw the pilot shaking his head, and Mark and Teresa yelled at him furiously.

Then they flew off.

They left me.

"WHAT KIND OF RESCUE HELICOPTER LEAVES A KID IN THE MIDDLE OF A BUNCH OF YETIS?!"

All he had to do was throw me a rope. I would've hung on all the way to town if I had to.

They had to come back and get me.

They had to.

Teresa and Mark wouldn't let them forget about me, would they?

I felt doomed. I knew how long it took to get

a helicopter up there the first time. I'd missed out. They'd forgotten about me.

Then out of nowhere came my voice of reason.

The rescue chopper wasn't prepared for a bunch of yetis.

If that pilot would've tried to stay in the air, they would've crashed. If they landed, the yetis would've torn them apart.

They'd send another helicopter eventually. At least I hoped they would.

Without anything to defend myself, I was pretty desperate when the yeti burst through the attic door.

As the beast struggled to pull itself through the remains of the door, a beam of light fell on its head and made it howl.

The sun.

The only thing that could've possibly pulled my attention away from my attacker slipped through the clouds overhead. It cast an orange glow over the attic, forcing me to squint a bit to refocus on the monster.

When the bright light hit its face, the thing's growl curdled a bit, and it threw up its arm to block out the sun's rays.

Its eyes dimmed.

The red glow became nothing more than two pen lights.

While the yeti stood distracted, I took what I figured was my only chance to escape.

Hopping the boxes, I ran to the window.

Its footsteps . . . it was right behind me.

With no time to size up the drop and no time to even get scared . . .

I jumped out of the window.

One of the craziest feelings of my life had to be falling through the air down into a sea of whiteness. It felt like I'd leaped off the page of what was real, and down into a huge, expansive void.

Nothing.

Until I hit the canopy covering the wood pile outside. The canvas acted like a trampoline, sending me back into the air and dropping me on the ground.

The snow wasn't deep enough to keep me from hitting the earth. My knees plunged through, onto Uncle Shoe's lawn. One knee found a rock. That hurt the worst. The other pain came from the shock of landing in the yard's thick, icy covering.

Without the snow to cushion my fall a bit, I would've been trashed. That still didn't mean everything was okay, though. Jumping into four feet of snow wearing only a sweatshirt and blue jeans means you're going to freeze your rear end off.

It also wakes you up.

I got to my feet and found my senses working double time.

I heard the yeti at the attic window roaring down at me.

I tasted a little blood in my mouth and touched the huge, swelling knot on my knee.

Beside me, I smelled the two-toned charcoal beast that'd attacked the helicopter and paid for it.

And I saw . . . well, I saw everything.

From the shadows inside the house, a bunch of the creatures began to emerge, snarling and slapping about like they couldn't believe I'd gotten out of the house. They came from the woods, too, and I realized that these things must've covered the whole mountain.

I saw . . .

The sun sank lower, preparing to vanish all together behind the trees. The snow was still falling, just a little bit, and I knew that if the sun disappeared, the storms would start again. I had to escape now.

I saw . . .

Old Thunder Blades lying exactly where it had been tossed. I'd found my ticket out of there.

26

Favoring my good leg, I struggled back over to the side of the house to recover the sled, kicking my bad knee out to the side to lessen the weight on it.

The yetis were coming.

I heard the one from the attic jump, and land in the snow just a few feet behind me as I reached the outer wall of the house.

When I grabbed the sled, another one from inside the house reached through the window and tried to grab my neck.

The ones coming out of the woods had flanked my right side.

I hobbled out of the yard and into the woods on the other side of the house, pulling the sled along. Behind me I could hear the crashing of the monsters leaving the house.

And coming after me.

I darted around each and every tree that got in my way. The blades of the sled kept knocking against my hurt knee, and taking the time to switch hands forced me to slow down for just an instant.

That's all the time the monsters needed to jump down from the trees.

One dropped to my left and went for my head with its swinging claw.

I didn't stop to confront it at all. I just ducked to avoid it while I sprinted by.

More yetis jumped from the trees but I managed to stay a few steps ahead of them.

With the beasts so close behind me, I didn't have to worry about what decision to make.

I had only one choice.

Running in the only direction I could, I knew where I'd end up, and what I'd have to do.

And as I broke out of the woods into the open lip of snow just above the drop, I stared wide-eyed at my challenge.

There it was.

The Cut.

27

The yetis were making even more noise now.

The closer I came to the gorge, the less organized and focused they became.

All it took to get away, I hoped, would be jumping the crevice.

The Cut, I thought. *The rocky chasm looked like a gaping wound in the mountain. That's where the name came from.*

The creatures burst from the woods and my time ran out. I had to go down now.

Holding Uncle Shoe's old sled out in front of me, I launched myself off the top of the hill.

As I hit the snow, I almost screamed out in pain. My knee throbbed with every knock it took.

I heard a claw come down behind me. I

looked over my shoulder, and saw them pouring from the woods. Some of them were leaping in the air, others screaming in frustration.

I almost lost my balance as I bounced over the first rock. The blade popped up and I had to press my weight hard against that side to set it back down.

The monsters jumped, and landed in the snow on every side. Some rolled to their feet and lunged for the sled, but I'd built up my speed by then.

I kept my eyes on the rocks.

Dodge.

Turn.

Yeti!

A hard pull to the right got me away from it, and I thought I had a clear shot . . . until something grabbed my ankle.

MY KNEE . . .

I've never felt such agony. It yanked my entire leg.

It would've had me there except . . .

It happened to be ol' Peg Leg, the yeti I'd stabbed in the ankle.

The monster's foot was in no condition to

support a body trying to drag me to a stop. Peg Leg lost its balance, and slid down the hill behind me.

But now my speed had seriously decreased.

The gorge was just a few feet away.

I'd never make it.

I didn't have enough speed.

I'd be killed.

Unless I found a ramp to help me clear the gorge.

That's when I saw it.

A white lump at the edge of the drop.

Could be a rock, I hoped, *or it might just be a pile of snow.*

If it was a pile of snow I was still dead.

But if it wasn't . . .

I braced myself for the biggest gamble of my life, and steered the sled to it.

I hit the snow bank.

With my eyes wide open, I flew into the air.

28

I didn't look down.

I never took my eyes off the other side.

If there were any secrets lying at the bottom of that gorge, I never saw them.

When I finally crash-landed on the other side, I swore that'd be my last time crossing The Cut.

BLAM!

The sled stuck in the ground like a shovel, piercing my big, yellow inner tube on the other side and deafening me with its explosive burst.

I flew off upside down, with my feet in the air.

My head burrowed through the snow and found the hard earth underneath.

WHAM!

I popped right up on my feet in a spinning daze.

Turning around, I saw Peg Leg trying desperately to stop himself, but he slid face first right off into the chasm, screaming all the way down.

The other yetis managed to come to rolling stops.

My head was spinning. I couldn't keep my balance, and fell to the ground.

Everything swirled around and my head pounded with pulsing pain waves. But no matter how bad it hurt, I wouldn't take my eyes off of the creatures. Completely at their mercy, I waited for them to start leaping over the gorge to come and tear me to pieces.

It didn't happened.

Instead, they looked into the air.

The snow had practically stopped.

Then they turned their attention to me again. That's when the strangest thing of all happened.

One by one, they began to fade away.

Like images from a faulty movie projector, their substance began to vanish.

I'm not sure how long it took, but in a little longer than an instant, they had all disappeared.

I was too shocked to utter a word. Still on the verge of passing out because of the head wound I'd received in the crash, I convinced myself quickly that I wasn't imagining things.

I gave one last look at the other side of The Cut. Then I glanced over at my uncle's sled.

The claw marks had disappeared.

I actually tried to question it out loud, but finally succumbed to unconsciousness.

Everything went from white to black.

29

I woke up to find Teresa, Mark, and Uncle Shoe standing over me.

"What happened?" I moaned, instantly aching all over.

"You drove your head into the ground," Mark said.

"You've been out for about an hour." Teresa looked all teary-eyed. "Fortunately, we found you a few moments after you crashed, otherwise you would have frozen to death."

I lifted myself up to find we were bouncing around in what looked like an ambulance.

"Are you okay, my boy?" Uncle Shoe had his head wrapped in bandages.

"Where were you?" He knew it'd be my first question.

"I saw the monsters, Max. I saw the Abominable Snowmen. And they saw me. They attacked my truck halfway down the mountain. I tried to shake 'em off, but instead I lost control, and slammed that old truck of mine into a tree. A rescue team picked me up not long after that. I'd been fighting a head wound, too, but once I regained consciousness I started screaming about you kids, and they told me they'd already gotten your call," Uncle Shoe explained.

"They made the claw mark on your sled. How long have you known about them?" When I asked, my uncle didn't look so much surprised as he did relieved. He'd wanted to tell someone.

"I saw my first one on that day I told you about, the day after that big snow. It became my life after that. That's why I lived here in the mountains. I wanted to see one again. I wanted to prove that something like that could be real."

My head ached worse from all of the information I tried to cram into it. "So you knew they were here all along." It was a statement, not a question.

"Max, I couldn't prove it. I never saw another one since then until yesterday, when one hopped on my hood and shrieked at me."

"No one has any proof the things are even up there," Teresa said. "The helicopter pilot's been showing everyone what it did to his chopper, and they'll really freak when they see the damage to Uncle Shoe's house, but we don't have any evidence of the yetis. We don't have pictures, a footprint, or anything."

"The police will check it out! If this many people saw them, how could they not take it seriously?" Mark stressed.

"They'll never find them," I said. "I saw them disappear."

Teresa and Mark looked at me, and then to my injured head.

"No. Really. They vanished. They just faded away, right before my eyes."

Uncle Shoe smiled.

"What were they, Uncle Shoe?! They weren't just animals! Not with those eyes! Not when they can just disappear like that! And the snow . . . as soon as they were gone, it stopped too. What were they?!" I wanted to know so bad I wasn't even aware I was yelling.

Uncle Shoe leaned in even closer than he already was. "If something's there one second and then fades away, what do you call it? Things glowing in the dark and appearing out of nowhere . . . things you could've sworn were real but were only there under a haunting circumstance. I can only think of one thing to call them."

"Ghosts?"

"Yes. I believe so. I think they haunt that piece of land around my home."

"Why did you leave us there if you knew that?" Mark asked.

"I never knew for sure. It was my only explanation for something that happened to me fifty years ago. I saw one then. It attacked my sled, and then disappeared. It's funny though, I never noticed the claw marks until Max pointed them out."

I knew it. But I couldn't blame Uncle Shoe. He didn't want to tell us something that he knew would scare us and that he wasn't one hundred percent sure of in the first place. He really had no proof except what he saw. If he didn't reach his sled fast enough after the yeti attacked it,

115

the claw marks would've disappeared. They only reappeared when the yetis were about to come back.

"But why do they haunt that part of the mountain? What makes it so special?" Teresa asked.

"Well, I've done a little book digging and I think that gorge is the answer. Over a hundred years ago when Crier Mountain was nameless and its resources were just being explored, a freak blizzard trapped a group of miners at the bottom of the ravine. They all froze to death. Their ghosts come back to haunt that area."

"And anyone close by," Mark added.

Uncle Shoe nodded.

"So, you're telling me the yetis are ghosts that control the snowstorms by themselves?"

Uncle Shoe shook his head.

"You've got it all wrong, Max. Like I said, I haven't seen these things in fifty years, but one thing is constant between the two instances, and it will be a tell-tale sign for the future."

"What? What is it?"

"They didn't bring the storm, Max. The storm brought them."

30

I spent the rest of my vacation sitting on the couch while all of my friends enjoyed what remained of the biggest snow Fairfield had gotten in fifty years.

Nothing else could have felt as good.

Mark stayed on the phone most of the time, reciting our adventure to people who had heard about a crisis on Crier Mountain.

Surprisingly, Teresa hadn't called anyone at all. Out of the three of us, she was the only one who decided to have some fun in the snow. She possibly felt that the best way to confront bad memories would be to have snowball fights.

As for me, I opted for a good book.

Uncle Shoe had been visiting friends in town all week (with his house in the shape it was in, it would be a little tough for him to keep to him-self), and he came by our house often. He kept wanting to bring me things to make up for the whole torturous experience. Anyway, I only asked him for one book.

The Almanac.

I'd find the biggest storms expected for the next few years.

And I'd be on the lookout.

From my spot inside, I had a good view of the window.

I watched the last flakes of Fairfield's worst snowstorm ever fall to the ground . . .

Until next season.

And now
an exciting preview
of the next

STRANGE MATTER™

#9 Deadly Delivery
by Marty M. Engle

There's one in every town.

Some are tall, leaning relics perched high on wind-blown hills. Others squat on barren streets like hollow shells of grey wood and broken glass.

From deserted lighthouses on shrouded shorelines, to empty stone towers in long-dead fields, they lure the curious in with hushed secrets.

They know stories so dreadful and terrifying that if you heard them, it would freeze your blood, or turn your hair snow white.

All over the world, they wait patiently, ready to catch unwary visitors, never to release them again.

Haunted houses.

I have a terrifying story about a haunted house at 331 Sycamore Street in Fairfield.

It's a nice, beige, three bedroom in a quiet

cul-de-sac with towering trees overhanging a huge backyard, with a leaf-filled tarp covering a pool.

My house.

It all started one stormy, rainy night in October as I hurriedly finished yet another award-winning cartoon. Sitting at the crowded desk in my room, I sketched and drew, wiping away the eraser dust from another masterpiece.

This one turned out awesome.

Wait! One final touch. I pushed the pencil across the rounded head, swirling and swirling in a gentle arc until a perfect nest of hair sat on top of my prize creation, COOL DOG YAK! My absolute best character, and the subject of an ongoing, underground success story at Fairfield Junior High, seventh grade.

He's got a hot dog body, simple face, and stick arms and legs: crude but effective. His speciality is mocking teachers and destroying a cartoon version of the infamous Kyle Banner in gross and disgusting ways. That's what made my strip so popular in class. Everyone loves seeing Kyle get his. But he deserves it for all the terror he dishes out. I'm talking about rubber band whelps the size of golfballs, books drop kicked out of three-story windows, and humiliating public thrashings for reasons known only to him.

COOL DOG YAK stands up for what's right and gives Kyle exactly what he deserves. Everyone thinks I draw Kyle perfectly; that I have him down to a science. It's no wonder.

He lives next door.

I ran to the wall and pinned my latest and greatest up with the rest of cartoons.

Glancing through my curtain and the rain to the house next door, I saw no sign of movement from Kyle's bedroom window.

I knew the chance of Kyle seeing those drawings from his window was remote, but I could never be too careful. As far as I knew, he hasn't even heard about them.

No one at school has told Kyle or shown him the cartoons. Everyone has been extra careful to keep it an absolute secret, ensuring my safety and their entertainment. I didn't want to think about what would happen if he ever saw one of my cartoons. They'd probably never find my body.

"SIMON! MOM'S ON THE PHONE!" Sarah yelled from downstairs.

Sarah is my twin sister. She helps me pass the cartoon out to the class, at extreme risk to her own life. Kyle acknowledges no difference between boys and girls, only that they should fear him equally.

Sarah could probably talk her way out of a thrashing if she had to. She's a great speaker and reader, and always gets the highest scores in oral reports. She's kind of a brain, but everyone likes her because she's so nice all the time. She's almost too nice.

We look so much alike, it creeps some people out. Because of our super bright-blue eyes and white-blond hair, people tell us we look like dolls or like the kids in that old movie, *Village of the Damned*. They treat us like we're mind-linked or something.

"SIMON!" Sarah yelled again.

"WHAT DOES SHE WANT?" I yelled back, hanging out of my bedroom door.

"SHE WANTS TO TALK TO YOU!"

Great. Mom and Dad had gone over to the Donaldsons' about three hours before. They always wound up going to somebody's house on Friday nights. "We'll be back by nine," Mom said. Now it was ten-thirty.

I bounced down the last three steps and saw the phone hung on its stand in the foyer.

"Why'd you hang up?" I yelled.

The rain outside had really started to come down. I could see sheets of water running down the frosted glass windows that framed the front door.

"Mom had to go. She just wanted us to know they were going to be very late," Sarah said, stepping in from the living room.

She was still holding her prized journal. That little diary held every thought, every secret, every hope she had. She carried it around everywhere and wrote in it everyday. It's practically her best friend.

"Should we ground them?" I joked.

"You'll definitely want to. She said Ms. Glower's coming over in an hour."

"WHAT! Oh, no. WHY? We're too big for a sitter. How old does she think we are? We're not babies! We can take care of ourselves!"

A crack of lightning flashed outside.

The lights flickered and dimmed, then sputtered back on.

"Uh, oh. The power's going to go," Sarah said, peering up at the domed light in the hallway ceiling.

"Yeah, maybe. So what? We're twelve years old for Pete's sake! Why did Mom go and do that?"

Another crack of lightning flashed with a thundering boom that sounded like it came from just outside the door, startling us, making us jump.

"Whoa. Did you feel that?" Sarah asked, her eyes widening.

"Yeah. Again. So what? It's just a stupid storm. I'll get the flashlight if the power goes out."

"I'm just glad Ms. Glower will be here soon," Sarah muttered, obviously comforted by the thought.

"Oh, give me a break. Not you, too! We are perfectly capable of staying alone."

The rain pounded hard on the roof of the house. The lights flickered again as a shrill wind rattled the windows in their frames.

"We know all the routines! The police number, the fire number, the number of the neighbors," I ranted, waving my arms about. "Don't do this. Don't do that. Don't talk on the phone if there's lightning outside."

The rain fell harder, in heavy sheets.

"Don't stand too close to windows if the wind is blowing too hard."

The wind blew stronger, whipping against the windows with a shrill whistle.

"And the everr-popular: don't open the door to strangers."

The doorbell rang.

I stopped my ranting. We looked at the door stunned, as if it rang on cue.

The doorbell rang again.

"No way," I whispered.

"Who? Ms. Glower?" Sarah asked.

We froze in place. No way Ms. Glower could have gotten over her this fast if Mom had just called her. We both knew it.

"I don't think so," I gulped.

The doorbell rang again as a deafening clap of thunder shook the house.

The lights blew out, plunging us into total darkness.

My heart nearly flew from my chest. Sarah gasped, clutching me. "Simon, the window! Look!"

Another flash of lightning lit the skinny windows beside the door, revealing the huge, hulking shape of a man, right outside the door, swaying back and forth . . .

Trying to peer inside.

The doorbell rang again.

About the Authors

Marty M. Engle and **Johnny Ray Barnes Jr.**, graduates of the Art Institute of Atlanta, are the creators, writers, designers and illustrators of the **Strange Matter**® series and the **Strange Matter**® **World Wide Web page.**

Their interests and expertise range from state of the art 3-D computer graphics and interactive multi-media, to books and scripts (television and motion picture).

Marty lives in La Jolla, California with his wife Jana and twin terror pets, Polly and Oreo.

Johnny Ray lives in Tierrasanta, California and spends his free time with his fiancée, Meredith.